Five Enormous Dinosaurs

illustrated by **Will Bonner**

Child's Play (International) Ltd
Ashworth Rd, Bridgemead, Swindon SN5 7YD, UK
Swindon   Auburn ME   Sydney
© 2018 Child's Play (International) Ltd   Printed in Heshan, China
ISBN 978-1-78628-177-7   HH131117NBH01181777
1 3 5 7 9 10 8 6 4 2
www.childs-play.com

Five enormous dinosaurs, letting out a roar.

ROAR!

ROAR!

One stomped away...

Four enormous dinosaurs, knocking down a tree.

One stomped away...

...and then there were three.

Stomp! Stomp!
Stomp! Stomp!
Stomp! Stomp!
Stomp! Stomp!
ROAR!

Three enormous dinosaurs, eating veggie stew.

One stomped away...

Two enormous dinosaurs, resting in the sun.

One stomped away...

...and then there was one.

Stomp! Stomp!
Stomp! Stomp!
Stomp! Stomp!
Stomp! Stomp!
ROAR!

One enormous dinosaur, left all alone.

One stomped away...

No more dinosaurs letting out a roar!

One enormous dinosaur
so very, very old!

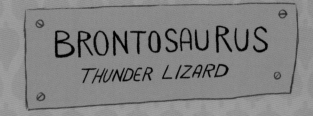

BRONTOSAURUS
THUNDER LIZARD

Stomp! Stomp! Stomp! Stomp! Stomp! Stomp!

Stomp! Stomp! ROAR!

Spinosaurus

Carnotaurus

Suchomimus

Tyrannosaurus Rex

Triceratops

Coelophysis Bauri

Brontosaurus

Stegosaurus

Ankylosaurus